DATE DUE

DISCARD

PRINTED IN U.S.A.

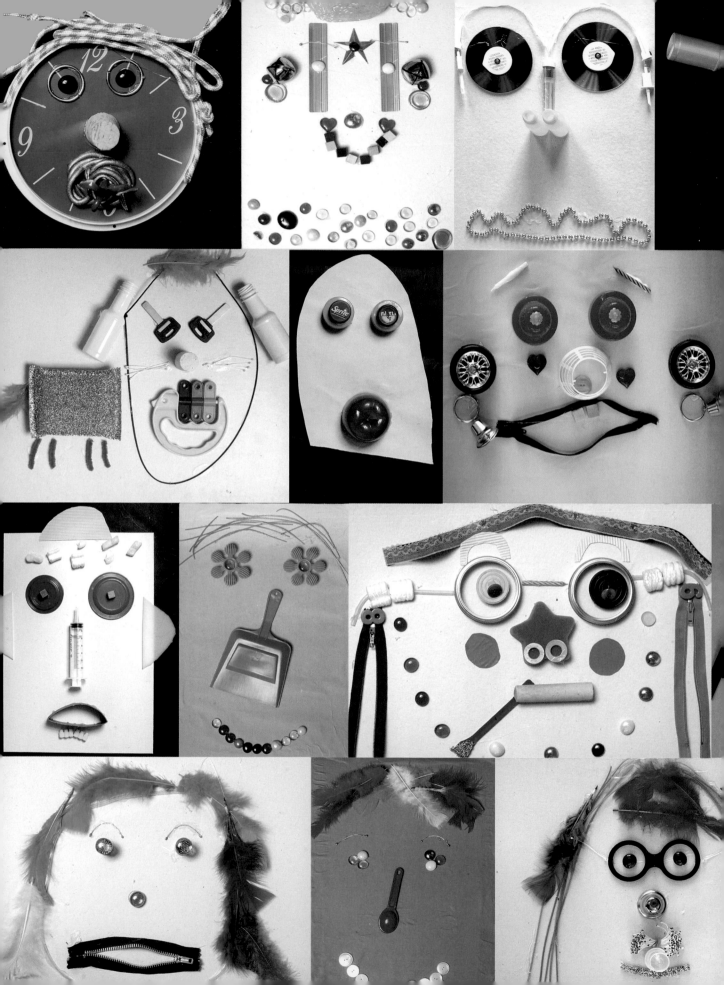

Author's Note

In January 2006, I spent three inspiring and unforgettable days in the oncology department at the Schneider Children's Medical Center of Israel, conducting workshop sessions with children and teenagers who were sick with cancer. The workshop was called "Drawing with Objects." The kids created self-portraits and portraits of their families using objects found in everyday life, as well as items from the hospital. The pictures made by the younger children appear—with many thanks—on the endpapers. This book is dedicated to them.

Text and cover and interior illustrations copyright © 2007 by Hanoch Piven

All rights reserved. Published in the United States by Dragonfly Books, an imprint of Random House Children's Books, a division of Random House, Inc., New York. Originally published in hardcover in the United States by Schwartz & Wade Books, an imprint of Random House Children's Books, New York, in 2007.

Dragonfly Books with the colophon is a registered trademark of Random House, Inc.

Visit us on the Web! randomhouse.com/kids

Educators and librarians, for a variety of teaching tools, visit us at randomhouse.com/teachers

The Library of Congress has cataloged the hardcover edition of this work as follows:
Piven, Hanoch.
My dog is as smelly as dirty socks: and other funny family portraits/Hanoch Piven.
— 1st ed.
p. cm.
Summary: A young girl draws a family portrait, then makes it more accurate by adding common objects to show aspects of each member's personality, such as her father's playfulness, her mother's sweetness, and her brother's strength.
ISBN 978-0-375-84052-4 (tr.) — ISBN 978-0-375-94052-1 (lib. bdg.)
[1. Portraits—Fiction. 2. Individuality—Fiction. 3. Family life—Fiction.] I. Title.
PZ7.P68943My 2007
[E]—dc22
2006021936

ISBN 978-0-307-93089-7 (tr. pbk.)

MANUFACTURED IN CHINA

10 9 8 7 6 5 4 3 2 1

First Dragonfly Books Edition

Random House Children's Books
supports the First Amendment
and celebrates the right to read.

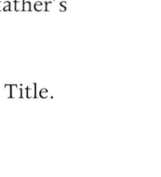
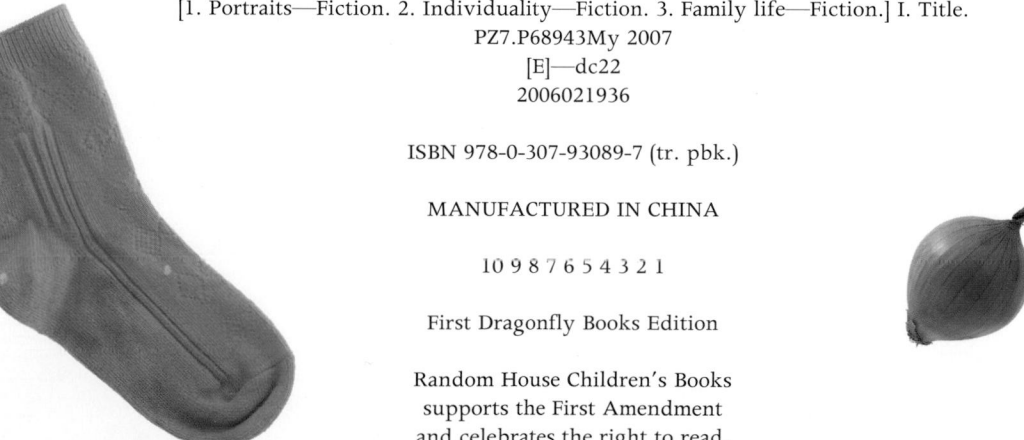

My Dog is as Smelly as Dirty Socks

AND OTHER FUNNY FAMILY PORTRAITS
BY HANOCH PIVEN

Dragonfly Books ———→ New York

MY BIG
BROTHER

MY DADDY   MY
                MOMMY

MY BABY BROTHER

ME

AND
SCHMUTZ

My teacher asked me to draw a picture of my family, and this is what I drew.

I showed it to her and she said, **"How great is that!"**

But I didn't like it.

Look at my dad.

There are so many things
about him that you don't
see in this picture.

Like . . .

My daddy is as
jumpy as a SPRING

and as playful as a
SPINNING TOP.

He is as fun as a
PARTY FAVOR.

But sometimes he's as stubborn
as a KNOT in a ROPE.

So I made my
picture better, see?

That's *him*!

(Isn't he nutty?)

And what about
this drawing of
my mom?

Sorry, but it doesn't
tell the whole story.

My mommy is as soft
as the softest FLUFF

and as bright as
the brightest LIGHT.

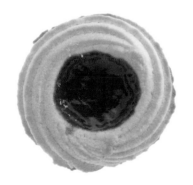

She is as tasty as the
crunchiest COOKIE.

No, TASTIER!
She's as delicious
as a CROISSANT.

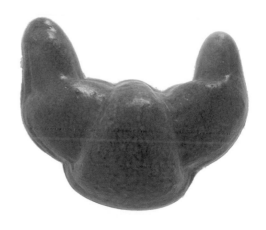

That's my yummy mommy!

(Mommy, I'm going to eat you all up.)

And now you're
probably wondering
what my big brother
is *really* like.

Well . . .

My brother is as amusing as a game of MARBLES

 and as strong as a BASEBALL BAT,

but when we play hide-and-seek, he's as sneaky as a SNAKE.

Oh, and one more thing:
He eats like a . . .

(I'll give you a clue: "Oink, oink.")

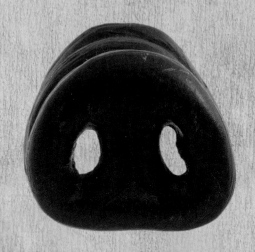

...PIG!

That's my brother
right there.

And what about
my baby brother?

He is not this quiet.

My baby brother is as sweet as CANDY (this is true).

But he never stops crying!

 He's as loud as a WHISTLE,

or maybe a HORN,

 or even an ALARM CLOCK.

No, LOUDER! He's as loud as a FIRE TRUCK.

Isn't he cute?
Now, SHHHHH!!!

And then there
is Schmutz.

I'll be honest with you . . .
Schmutz stinks!

Schmutz is as stinky
as an ONION.

He's as nasty
as canned FISH,

as icky as PEPPERONI,

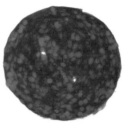

and as smelly as
DIRTY SOCKS.

(Turn the page at your own risk. . . .)

YUCKY-BOO!

(I warned you.)

But what about me?

Well, there is
SOOOOOOOO
much I want to tell you
about me!

I am a princess,

as majestic as a CROWN

 and as sugary as a JELLY BEAN.

I am as sharp as a PENCIL

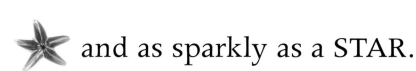

and as sparkly as a STAR.

(Wait—I have more!)

 I am as colorful as a FLOWER

and as lovely as PERFUME.

 I am as strong as a STONE

and as good as an ANGEL.

(Hey! I'm not done yet.)

I am as funny as a tickly FEATHER

and as curious as
a MAGNIFYING GLASS.

I am faster than a CALCULATOR

and all around, as special as
BEACH GLASS.

But more important than all of that . . .

My heart is BIG . . .

and with it,
I love my special
family.

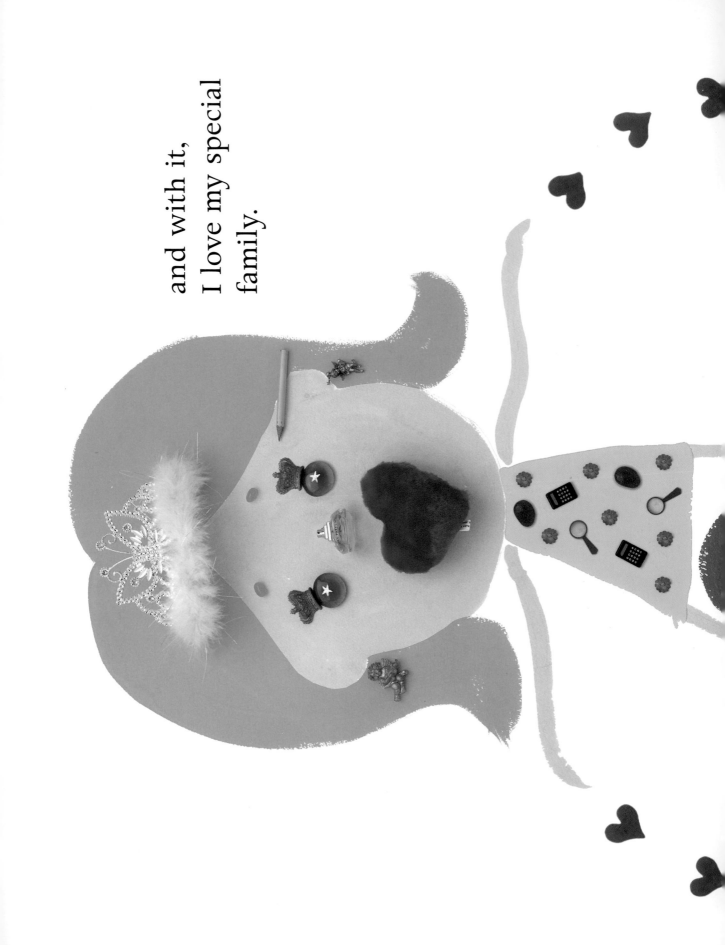

Now tell me about *your* special family. What do they look like?

Here's a list of objects that can help you think about how to make portraits of your family:

Things that say "smart":
ruler, numbers, owl

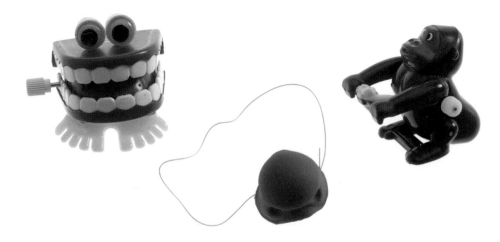

Things that say "funny":
chattering teeth, clown nose, toy monkey

Things that say "scratchy":
steel wool, sharp teeth, cactus

Things that say "soft":
teddy bear, cotton ball, slipper

Things that say "strong":
action figure, elephant, hammer

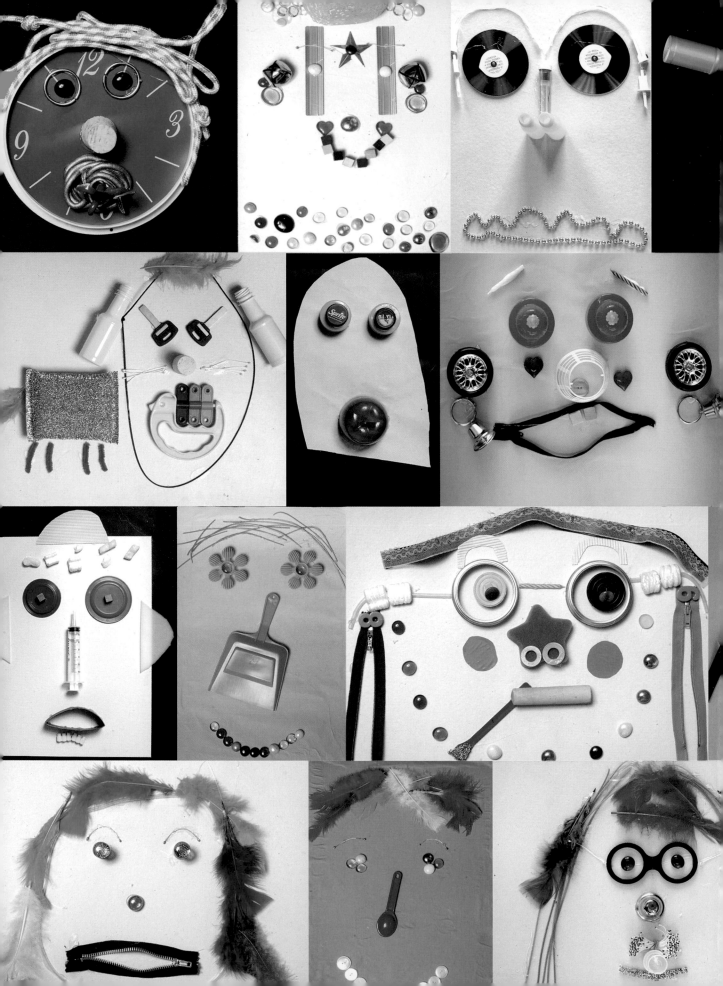

Don't miss
MY BEST FRIEND IS AS SHARP AS A PENCIL:
AND OTHER FUNNY CLASSROOM PORTRAITS,
also by Hanoch Piven

"Great, inventive fun." —*Kirkus Reviews*

"Vibrant portraits . . . will delight readers." —*Booklist*